www.randomhouse.com/kids
www.seussville.com
www.kohlscorporation.com

Educators and librarians, for a variety of teaching tools,
visit us at www.randomhouse.com/teachers

This special edition was printed for Kohl's by Random House Children's Books,
a division of Random House, Inc., New York.

ISBN-13: 978-0-375-84165-1
ISBN-10: 0-375-84165-2

PRINTED IN CHINA
10 9 8 7 6 5 4 3 2 1

Green Eggs and Ham

Ham

By Dr. Seuss

BEGINNER BOOKS
A Division of Random House, Inc.

That Sam-I-am!

That Sam-I-am!

I do not like

that Sam-I-am!

Do you like

green eggs and ham?

I do not like them,
Sam-I-am.
I do not like
green eggs and ham.

Would you like them
here or there?

I would not like them
here or there.
I would not like them
anywhere.
I do not like
green eggs and ham.
I do not like them,
Sam-I-am.

Would you like them
in a house?
Would you like them
with a mouse?

I do not like them
in a house.
I do not like them
with a mouse.
I do not like them
here or there.
I do not like them
anywhere.
I do not like green eggs and ham.
I do not like them, Sam-I-am.

Would you eat them
in a box?
Would you eat them
with a fox?

Not in a box.

Not with a fox.

Not in a house.

Not with a mouse.

I would not eat them here or there.

I would not eat them anywhere.

I would not eat green eggs and ham.

I do not like them, Sam-I-am.

Would you? Could you?

In a car?

Eat them! Eat them!

Here they are.

I would not,
could not,
in a car.

You may like them.
You will see.
You may like them
in a tree!

I would not, could not in a tree.

Not in a car! You let me be.

I do not like them in a box.

I do not like them with a fox.

I do not like them in a house.

I do not like them with a mouse.

I do not like them here or there.

I do not like them anywhere.

I do not like green eggs and ham.

I do not like them, Sam-I-am.

A train! A train!

A train! A train!

Could you, would you,

on a train?

Not on a train! Not in a tree!
Not in a car! Sam! Let me be!

I would not, could not, in a box.
I could not, would not, with a fox.
I will not eat them with a mouse.
I will not eat them in a house.
I will not eat them here or there.
I will not eat them anywhere.
I do not eat green eggs and ham.
I do not like them, Sam-I-am.

Say!

In the dark?

Here in the dark!

Would you, could you, in the dark?

I would not, could not,
in the dark.

Would you, could you,
in the rain?

I would not, could not, in the rain.

Not in the dark. Not on a train.

Not in a car. Not in a tree.

I do not like them, Sam, you see.

Not in a house. Not in a box.

Not with a mouse. Not with a fox.

I will not eat them here or there.

I do not like them anywhere!

You do not like

green eggs and ham?

I do not
like them,
Sam-I-am.

Could you, would you,
with a goat?

I would not,
could not,
with a goat!

Would you, could you,
on a boat?

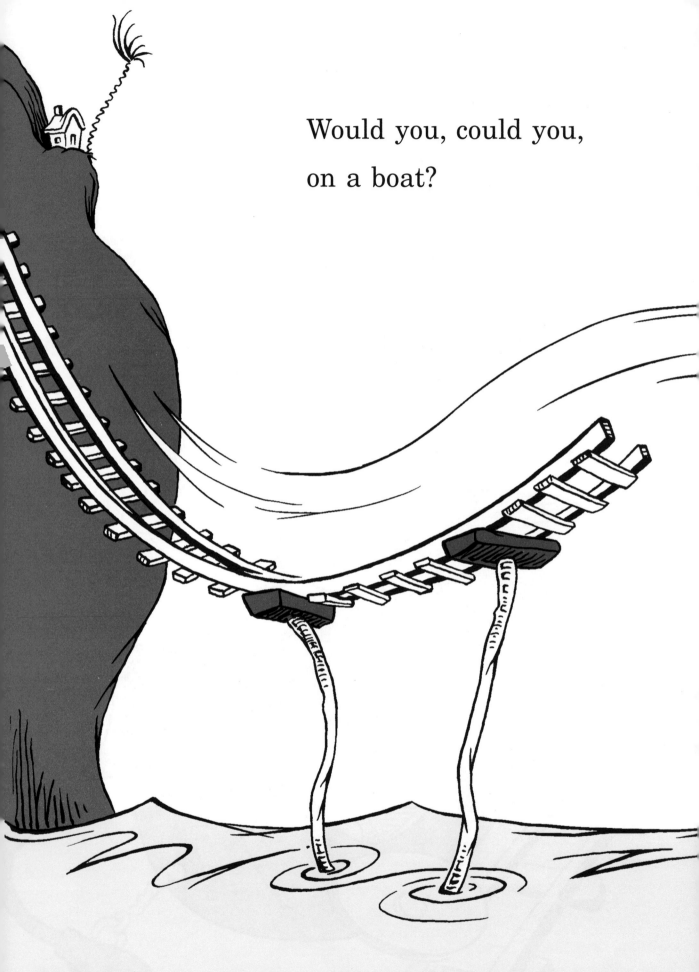

I could not, would not, on a boat.

I will not, will not, with a goat.

I will not eat them in the rain.

I will not eat them on a train.

Not in the dark! Not in a tree!

Not in a car! You let me be!

I do not like them in a box.

I do not like them with a fox.

I will not eat them in a house.

I do not like them with a mouse.

I do not like them here or there.

I do not like them ANYWHERE!

I do not like
green eggs
and ham!

I do not like them,
Sam-I-am.

You do not like them.

So you say.

Try them! Try them!

And you may.

Try them and you may, I say.

Sam!

If you will let me be,

I will try them.

You will see.

Say!

I like green eggs and ham!

I do! I like them, Sam-I-am!

And I would eat them in a boat.

And I would eat them with a goat . . .

And I will eat them in the rain.

And in the dark. And on a train.

And in a car. And in a tree.

They are so good, so good, you see!

So I will eat them in a box.

And I will eat them with a fox.

And I will eat them in a house.

And I will eat them with a mouse.

And I will eat them here and there.

Say! I will eat them ANYWHERE!

I do so like
green eggs and ham!
Thank you!
Thank you,
Sam-I-am!